I0749194

DILLY TREE BOOKS
Dilly Tree Publishing • Atlanta

Ámbudan was my Friend

DILLY
TREE

Ámbudan was my Friend

Poetry and Prose

By

Sam "SIP SIP" Williams

DILLY TREE BOOKS

Dilly Tree Publishing • Atlanta

DILLY TREE BOOKS
Published by Dilly Tree Publishing

All works original by Sam "SIP SIP" Williams,
also known as R. Samuel Williams, Jr.

Published in the United States of America by
Dilly Tree Books, an imprint of Dilly Tree Publishing,
both subsidiaries of SIP SIP STUDIOS, LLC.,
Atlanta, Georgia.

www.thedillytree.com

Library of Congress Cataloging-in-Publication Data
Ámbudan was my Friend / A Collection of Poems and Prose
by Sam "SIP SIP" Williams

ISBN 978-0-9816424-4-4

Cover Illustration & Jacket Design by the Author.
Printed & Manufactured in the United States of America
by Lightning Source, Inc., LaVergne, Tennessee

First Edition: June 2008
Second Edition: January 2024

PUBLISHER'S NOTE
Portions of this book are non-fictional.
In particular instances, names, characters, places and incidents
have been modified for the protection of identity.

To:

Bev, Crystal, Sam Jr., Candice,
&
Soldier

Also to:
Leviticus "Uncle Lou" Adderley
Sonja Knowles
Mrs. Morfydd William
Richard Standen

This book is also a memorial to:

Annamae Jane Bootle-Williams

Rupert Alexander Williams

Table of Contents

ACKNOWLEDGEMENTS	xii
INTRODUCTION	xiv

GENERAL POETRY - PART I

THE VALLEY	20
MARISSA	21
NATURE WALK	22
ÁMBUDAN WAS MY FRIEND	23
FANCY	28
IF I GROW UP	30
I NEED SOME MONEY	33
THE NOBODIES	35
TIRED	37
WHEN I DIE	38
CHILDREN OF SUICIDE	40
ON BEING POOR	42
CHERISH	44
MY HERO	45
ANNA JANE	47

PART II

INSIGHTED	50

THE OPPONENT 51

BARRED 54

INSTANTANEOUS 56

DEFENCE OF GORGEOUS 59

UNION DUES 60

SMOKIN' BETSY 63

WHY? 65

LIFELONG TORMENT 67

THE KITE 68

TEACHER'S PET 71

OLE RUPE 72

PART III

BOTTOM LINE 76

HEARTSTRING 77

HALLOWED CAVITY 79

THE RUDDER 80

RAGE OF FOOLS 81

MIND SPIN 82

WASTELAND 84

THE PAUPER 85

LOVE OF HATRED 86

GIMME DAT 87

MOODY 89

SEARCH FOR TRUTH 91

RAT STANDARD 92
THE INNOCENT ONE 93
SURPRISE 94
TRIALS OF ANNA 95
TRAVELLING TEACHERS 98

PART IV

FATHOM 100
TELL ME 101
LAPSE 102
SHAKEDOWN 103
LAW OF LOVE 106
JUGULAR SOCIETY 107
LEGALLY ILLEGAL 111
THE MACHINERY 113
NOWHERELAND 115

SOCIOPOLITICAL POETRY - PART V

BORN TO DIE (10,000 FUNERALS) 118
BAHAMIAN DEMOCRACY 120
THE RETALIATION 121
FREEDOM SONG 123
SONG OF THE EXILE 125
WHY ARE THEY CRYING? 130
THE LAST STRAW 132
ABOUT THE AUTHOR 134

ACKNOWLEDGEMENTS

Over the years, the Lord has blessed me with a family that has been a bedrock of strength, and there is no amount of thanks that I can give to express my gratitude for their support, and their continued encouragement while completing this book.

My wife Bev was a driving force in bringing this collection to existence. When I told her that I was writing a book, she gave me “the look,” but as soon as I got the ball rolling, she in her classic nature, routinely checked to keep me in pace.

I had asked her not to read my manuscript until it was complete, yet one evening, I saw her peeking over my shoulder with a girlish blush as I worked. When I pulled away from her, she smiled, and told me to hurry up and finish.

This pretty much paints the backdrop of my life with respect to the arts, as she, along with my children, Crystal, Sam, Candice and Soldier, were central to my lifelong artistic ambitions, always providing a great latitude of support.

I acknowledge and thank my parents, my late mother Annamae, who passed away in 2003, and my father, “Daddy Rupe,” who passed away in November of 2023. It was such an honor and a comfort to read the poem “Ole Rupe” at his funeral, reflecting on his no-nonsense approach to education.

My sister, Dyla Ann Williams, is a children's book writer, and the passion that she showed while publishing her first book was a great motivation.

I am grateful to have been blessed with extremely gifted and selfless educators, particularly literature teachers and professors, who, during my development, took the time to nurture, advise, and criticize me, especially during the early years, when I began to read and write poetry. I remain particularly thankful to several university professors, who assisted me in obtaining opportunities to support my family while completing my university education.

I am forever grateful to the late Mr. Kenneth N. Francis, former Publisher of the Nassau Guardian, for the abundance of kindness shown to myself and my family, before and while attending university. I thank the Lord that our paths came together, and the impact that he had on both my life and career.

There are countless Bahamians, Americans and citizens of the world; friends and relatives; far too many to mention, who over the years, have contributed to this book by their very presence in my life. The lifelong lessons are appreciated.

Finally, I must thank the Lord God Almighty, for His grace, mercy, and blessings throughout the course of my life.

Sam "Sip Sip" Williams
January 2024

INTRODUCTION

I began to read and write poetry by sheer circumstance as a teenager, diving into it to fill in a void brought on by a troubling ordeal, mentioned in the poem *Barred.*

I had played hooky and ventured outside and got into trouble with young men from another neighborhood, passing through our neighborhood. This led to three months of banishment, which included staying late after school, and having my father pick me up from my "after school activities."

This spurred an interest in libraries, and one day, I ran across a book paying tribute to a lady called Gwendolyn Brooks, which celebrated the anniversary of her groundbreaking accomplishment of winning the Pulitzer Prize for poetry.

After reading that book, I had to find out first of all, what the Pulitzer was, and secondly, who was Gwendolyn Brooks. Finally, I had to find out just what was so spectacular about her poetry.

I vividly recall finding and reading her work, and then taking delightful pleasure in words that flowed and savored like melting butter, translating and transcending a universal commonality that I, like so many others, clearly identified with.

Finding the work of a black writer was a wonderful discovery. Prior to that, at the library at St.

Augustine's and at the public libraries in Nassau, I remember looking through numerous anthologies covering the greatest poets and poems ever written, and at that time there were no black poets in any of the collections which I read.

From there I stumbled into the Negritude Movement and writers of the Harlem Renaissance.

Up to that point, I had also become encompassed and well versed in the visual arts, studying the works and methods of the European Masters, particularly Jan Vermeer, whose techniques and curiously isolated path of life became an important influence. True artists show their work, not themselves. I was able to transfer the visual skills from my studies of drawing and painting, into my explorations of poetic word-crafting.

I was heavily influenced by my parents Rupert and Annamae Williams, who ran their home with a strict commitment to education.

From my early teens, I began to write about my life experiences, playing close attention and transferring concepts and ordeals into written notes and prose, especially those aspects which I regarded as critical pivotal nodes, which caused me to reconsider or redirect my life's path.

I enjoy repeating the fact that I was blessed with what I regard as dedicated and resourceful educators. Initially, I thought that my teachers would be offended that I would come to disrupt their lunch periods or breaks with questions about the poetry that I was reading, but was surprised and am grateful for their desire and eagerness to help.

A well accepted and basic tenet of poetry states that good poetry needs no explanation, and while my intent is to observe and obey that statute, I feel compelled to provide a backdrop to some of my work, as the background of many of the real-life settings are critical to the origin and concept.

One of the lessons that I discovered from my first edition of this book was that my cultural and social background themselves appeared to be a stumbling block which prevented outsiders from fully comprehending and appreciating my storylines. I am confident that the backdrops, which explain Bahamian colloquialisms, will not interfere with the reader's ability to explore and use their own imaginations toward an independent interpretation.

Ámbudan, the name within the book title, was one of my first experiences which led to critical thought, and stands as a structural template not just for my writing, but also for the way I live my life.

A number of poems relate to my family's experiences, particularly my mother and her turning blind several years before passing away.

Several poems reflect life in the southeastern United States, both as an immigrant as well as racially, after my arrival. *Born to Die* was written after a traumatic police stop on a rural Louisiana road.

Prior to coming to the United States, I had unassumingly completed the task of translating my teenage troubles onto the outer fringes of the real world political arena. After spending a little over a decade as a political cartoonist, I had, in a purely caricature, satirical and somewhat a cynical way, outlived my "unwelcome," in my native Bahamas, after a principalities fight with top powerbrokers.

The poem *Bahamian Democracy* was written at the peak of my frustration with the mechanics and social challenges of governance, and the concept of true democracy. Like several other poems, it reflects my then increasing contempt for political hypocrisy and double standards by those elected.

The Retaliation was written as an ode to four fallen Bahamian Defense Force heroes who were killed on HMBS Flamingo, during a Cuban military attack against the Bahamas. The ode represents a dynamic Machiavellian complex: the sacrifice of a few for the whole, where a theoretical act of retaliation, by actually not retaliating, is itself the greatest form of retaliation. **Absolute Sacrificial Puritanism.**

In today's age of warfare: Russia v Ukraine, and Hamas v Israel, such lessons in complex Absolute Sacrificial Puritanism, as displayed by the valiant Bahamian seamen, would lead to the betterment of mankind in general, and a more graceful and peaceful world.

Sam "Sip Sip" Williams
January 2024.

Great endowments often announce themselves in youth in the form of singularity and awkwardness.

- Johann Wolfgang Von Goethe

GENERAL POETRY

PART I

THE VALLEY

I was born in the valley
I grew up by the sea
While I confided in my Bible
My best friend was poverty

Learned to walk along the hillside
Climbed the mountains in my way
Watched the loners and the crooners
Kept my pace, earned my pay

Little older not much wiser
Upward climbing towards the top
Sky is cloudy, crowd getting rowdy
Nothing will slow me, make me stop

One day I'll sit back, tell my stories
Whirlwind started from a leaning shack
Like the world, tell my children
Reminisce about tailored facts

MARISSA

Marissa was a girl
From Nowhere Town
Cherubim face
Hair hung down
She shone a beauty
Never seen before

Young men
Approached her
With guarantees
She got her wants
She got her needs
Got a pocketbook
Full of broken lies

Slick suiters
Charmed her
With temporal deeds
Tongues of silver
Crushed glass for beads
Held a basket full
Of flowing tears

Oh Marissa
Why you aim so high
Jumped so high
Almost touched the sky
As you were falling
You fell so fast.

NATURE WALK

In sacred lands I stumbled,
Forest drenched in green;
What peace and joy I felt,
There, but yet not seen.

Humming island cedar trees,
Soothe, escape they bring;
Drowning out the city sounds,
Hypnotic breezes sing.

Nature shows her beauty,
Harmless; no danger zone;
Thirst quenched before you leave,
This springing precious home.

Tossing, turning, searching,
A soul confessing toil;
Before closed lids return to dust,
Each must return to soil.

ÁMBUDAN WAS MY FRIEND

Ámbudan was my friend

In all the years
I knew him
We never
Exchanged a word
Not a hearty hello
Nor a distant wave
Not even a solemn goodbye.

Had he sought
And fought
With me,
I could understand.
Had he grimaced
Scorned,
Or scoffed at me,
I could understand.

But there was nothing.
No exchange whatsoever…

Yet deep inside,
At the very core of my soul
I knew without a doubt
That indeed
Ámbudan was my friend.

* * * * * *

Rise up early,
Catch a lil' cowboy
Splash my face wit'
A bit o' cold water.
A dreadful Saturday morning
Shoe-shopping
Wit' Anna at Bells
Bound to be disastrous.

I had my mind set
On a sixteen dollar pair
Of spanking red high-top
Converse tennis shoes
The only thing she saw
Was a three dollar
Pair of "sweetwaters."
Generic!
Stink up a classroom
The first drop of rain!
I'll be stiff cold dead
'fore I wear one o' dem!

My first hand
At political negotiations.
An opponent wit' a serious case of the "cheepies"
Always claimin' to be broker than broke.
Sixteen Dollars?!
Sixteen Dollars?!
You mussy fool!
I gat six other chil'ren to feed!

She darted and shook
An eight dollar pair

Of white Dunlops
In my face.
This is it!

Dunlops? Dunlops?
Dunlop is a company that makes car tires!
She threw the Dunlops to the floor,
And raced towards the sweetwaters.
I grabbed the Dunlops, and ran to the cashier.

Dis woman head wasn't good.
Send me to St. Augustine's
'mongst dem uppity uppities
Wearin' a pair
Of car tires!

* * * * * *

Ten o'clock Monday morning
Suffocating beads of sweat
In the glistening Fox Hillian sun
P. E. class with Sharon and Martin
Layups on the confines
Of the open fenced courts.

Call-out time.
Everybody present,
Forty or so in all
Fully uniformed in sportswear.

Finally.
The last ten minutes.
The part we mostly enjoyed.

A free-for-all
Game of twenty-one.
Bodies jumpin' and bumpin' around
Reachin' for rebounds.

Something caught my eyes.

There he stood
A tall tower of intimidation
Masculine; strapping;
Ready to kick anyone's can.

I tried to ignore it
But he kept staring
At me, but not at me,
What was it?
I could feel it.
Staring at…

… my shoes?

The ball bounced past him,
I stopped in horror
Right in front of him
A cold hard lesson in reality.

At the base of this
Hovering colossal skyscraper
A pair of…
… bare feet.

Slowly, my eyes rose.
Panning vertically

Up this endless
Mountainous man,

Finally,
Face to face.
Then,
Eye to eye
Our solitary lifelong communication
No necessity to exchange words.

It was not a look
Of hatred or anger,
Neither was it a look of
Envy or indifference.

But more than a look
A yearning…

…Deep from the heart.

Someone who
Gladly would have
Given all
For a pair of...

Sweetwaters.

FANCY

don’t want no
fancy coffin
don’t want no
fancy suit

don’t want an
elaborate plot
or an
expensive
hidden boot

I want you to bury me naked
‘cause naked I came into this world,
and naked you kicked me out

bury me plain;
in the dirt
face down
cause that’s how
you treated me

‘round here with your pack o’ lies
‘bout I had my ways
but we were still close

you knew good an’ well
we hadn’t spoken in years
an’ none of us remembers why

so
if you're feeling kinda guilty
and need a second chance

if you
really
want to change

if you
really
          really
                    really
want to make a difference

instead of wasting
your time and money

on someone
who's dead

try spending it
on someone
who's living

IF I GROW UP

If I grow up
I wanna be
A fireman
Or maybe a policeman
A doctor or a lawyer
Or even
A politician.

It really
Doesn't matter
What I really wanna be
I got my whole future
In front of me

Fireman, fireman
Can you stop the burning?
Fireman, fireman
He said no.

Policeman, policeman
Can you stop the violence?
Policeman, policeman
She said no.

Doctor, doctor
Can you stop the bleeding?
Feel for the pulse
Answer yourself.

Politician, politician
Can you cure the country?
My brother, My Sister
Vote for me.

If I grow up
I wanna be
A baker
Or maybe a musician

A photographer or a painter
Or even
A preacher

Baker, baker
Is the cookie crumbling?
Baker, baker
He said yes

Musician, musician
Are we out of rhythm?
Musician, musician
She said yes.

Painter, painter
Is the picture fading?
Step back, take a look
Judge for yourself

* * * * * *

Preacher, preacher
Is our spirit dying?
Long lost child
Fall on your face
Humble yourself
And pray for grace
No matter who you are
No matter what you do
Stop pendin'
On people
To pull you through

If I grow up
All I want to be
Is someone
Not as naive as me.

I NEED SOME MONEY

I need some money!
I need some money!
I need some money!

Cuddled in my corner
On a Friday afternoon
I hear my baby cryin'
An' don't know what to do

I need some money!
I need some money!
I need some money!

The landlord took my earnin's
The shop-keeper took some too
Didn't gimme much groceries
That's exactly what he do!

Lord, where I goin'?
Lord, what ter do?
Only thing I know
It's a shame to be born so.

I need some money!
I need some money!
I need some money!

Preacher
Stop yer preachin!
Sister stop yer song!
Don’t tell dis growlin' belly
To lift its voice is wrong.

Generation pressure!
All I feel is stress!
Only the Good Lord knows
How to get me out o’ this.

I need some money!
I need some money!
I need some money!

THE NOBODIES

We are the nobodies
Masters of the Mind,
Victors of a volumous
Heap of nothingness.

Possessors of lowly estates,
Curators of our own universe,

We touch nothing,
We own nothing
We know nothing.

When we labor
We labor in vain
As we walk
We creep humbly in shame,

They neither see us
Hear us
Or want us.

But, when we cry,
We shout LOUD!!

A seldom boast
We strut PROUD!

To the tops of our voices
OH LORD!

OH LORD!
Deliver us.

At the close of day
We break bread and pray
And thank God

For our lives
And for our health

And our very breath
Is our pay.

TIRED

I'm tired.

Tired of struggling and toiling
In a world so confusin'
Endless paths with repeatin' constraints

Tired of lingerin' lines
Decrepit old minds
Singin' similar endless complaints

Tired of kickin' and knockin'
Tacklin' and blockin'
Of fightin' and 'fendin' my way.

Tired of limpin' and achin'
Bendin' and breakin'
And laborin' long for low pay.

Tired of friends who come fussin'
And bosses a cussin'
Of tunnels that never are lit.

Tired of long winding roads
And increasing dead loads -

I'm tired, but not too tired to quit.

WHEN I DIE

When I die
I don't want you
Standin' over my coffin
Screamin' an' hollerin'
Sobbin' an' sniffin'
Pretending
Like you cared.

Please,
Don't cry
Keep those tears
In your eyes

'cause
You know
And I know

Ain't none o' them real.

I remember,
Long ago,
When we began.

Together!
Committed to the cause!
All on the same side!

Or so I thought…
But…

When we tried to start;
You started your foolishness;

We tried to move;
You tried to move around me;

We began to do;
You began to do me in!

So
Please
Don't cry!

Please!
Please!
Please!

Don't cry!

Keep those tears,
In your eyes;

'cause
You know;
And
I know;

Ain't none o' them real.

CHILDREN OF SUICIDE

I wonder why
We turn blind eyes
Towards the brightness
Of the glaring sun.

Yesterday we were
Today we are
Forever ignorant
Of the mysterious unknown around us.

Idling in innocence
Cuddled in pride
We trod mightily
Into the perils of our past.

Deeper, deeper
Galloping steadily
Along a straight
Winding
Confusing path

Entangling
Strangling
Vigorous vines
Of self destruction

For we are
By our very nature

The children
Of suicide.

*   *   *   *   *   *

For Truth is Light

And the only ones
Who can look
Directly into the Light
Are the Blind.

ON BEING POOR

At night
I humble my way
Into a room full of darkness.
I see my children
Sprawled this way
And that way
Turning in the tirades of sleep
While I spin in the madness
Of my cyclic endeavors.

And I wonder
Is there any hope?
Is there any hope at all?
Skidding
Spiraling
Incessant discontentment

Trickling rays
Dawn teases the silence
Sunlight searching

I see a worn box spring
They eye a good mattress
I see four walls
They see a window
We all see the light
And wonder at the source

For our hopes
And nightmares
Are one

And come full daylight
They chase both fervently
Clutching one
Clubbing the other

For they are
An enlightened generation
Yearning,
Learning
Children of paupers
Fearless, furious
Casual, curious
Eventually, enviously
Admired.

*   *   *   *   *

The light fades
An encompassing darkness

And I wonder
Is there any hope?
Is there any hope at all...

For me?

CHERISH

Nothing to cherish
Like an early morning
Full of rebirth
Blooming spring
Crickets
Tobacco doves
Humming Hallowed Praises
Towards our God
In the Heavens

Mystery
Fate
Lurk beyond.

At random,
A friend
A foe...

Tomorrow knows…

MY HERO

In my heart
You're a hero
You stood
Strong in the fight
You fought for me
When I was weak
You took your
Blows in the battle

You're my
Modern version
Of Robin Hood
My freedom fighting
Le' Overture
My Martin
My Abe
My Sojourner Truth
And my galloping
Paul Revere

In my mind
You're a hero
Ignored the naysayers words
Gave your all
While asking for nothing
Just would not stop
Kept pressing ahead

When you left
My spirit fell
Now you're with God
Things are finally well

Fly high my song bird
Sing loud my song bird

Great lesson learned
I hold my head up high
I thank the Lord
For sending you my way
Big broken reed
You made the sacrifice
You believed in me when
I didn't believe in myself

ANNA JANE

I can still feel
The coral reef
Gnash against my knee
A mother's call
Burning Alcohol
Hurts so deep

I can tell the world
Keep your pity
Grew up hard
On the streets of Spring City

Every night
I heard
Anna pray

Did you hear
My mother call my name?
Did you hear
Her sweet sounding voice?
Calling out in prayer
Lord deliver my child
Did you hear, my mother pray?

I can still hear,
Ringing loud and clear
Rugged little wrestling boys
Push, shove and a bam!
Her favorite broken lamp

Stern loving, disciplined words

Calm quiet night
I hear her crying
Things gonna be all right

Every night
I heard
Anna pray

PART II

INSIGHTED

I've long stopped
Believing in blindness
And lost my
Comprehension of vision

Each passionate day
Another passing away
Of ideas
Ideals
Fading conventions

I awake
And hear what I can't see
To touch
To feel
An unreal dream

Eternal purging inside
Take the world on a ride

Dare to see
Close your eyes

INSIGHTED

THE OPPONENT

I never was
Much of a fighter
Not known for
Throwing blows
Never wanted to deck
Or put someone in check
No need to smash
Someone's face

Every King has
His pride
Gorgeous close
On the side
Time to stand
To protect
Time to garner respect
From kinsmen and foe
Even folk you don't know
It's about honor
About family
About posture

Then trouble came
Humility with shame
Unchartered predicament
Bashful ambivalence
Pulled in
By riotous
Foolish
Uprising

Awkward stance
Shoulders low
Nowhere to run
In defense of ignorance
Defeating senses
Without fighting
For wrong not worth righting
Holding the line
Against a fierce
Ferocious opponent

A stark illustration
Of brutish
Mindless
Stupidity

* * * * *

In latter days
The inevitable
Farsighted meeting
A dauntless
Wandering opponent
Pondering
Revenge

Yet this time
Something was different
A considerable change
Anxious craving
Squint in the distance
Behold
A startling surprise

An amazing
Smile and a wave

A theory
A thought
A conception

BARRED

Glistening bright morning
Sun on my face
A little weeze
A subtle cough
Fine day to stay home

Sharpen my lead strokes
Curve up my lines
Clothes and shoes bustling
Books and plates hustling
Fussing and struggling
To get them out the door

Then…
Absolute silence
Long yearned
Lonesome quietude
Wholesome solitude
A little sweet by myself

Need to stay still
Lay low
Can't blow my cover
She hasn't figured it out
Has she?

Just a bit more weezing
A teeny lil' more cough…

…Distant echo…
A bouncing ball
She's fast asleep

Hoop and call
An unpleasant surprise
Fellas from across town
Hookin' an' fakin'
Knockin' 'em down

Gotta defend my corner
Play and stand tall
Sharp piercing elbow
Embarrassing fall

Back in the game
Pride to defend
Show them my stuff
But elbowed again

Finally too much
Then stupidity kicked in
Arithmetic insanity
One against three
Pick and roll;

KAPOW!!!

Jump and run
Stupid, Stupid, Stupid
Could have been killed
Long term disappearance
Barred for three months

INSTANTANEOUS

ARRIVAL
***J*ourney**
***U*nforeseen**
***A*cceptance**
***T*ribulation**
***A*ttainment**
DEPARTURE
Regardless
Of level
Or Accomplishment

* * * * * * * *

There she stood
Stoic temple
Tortured embodiment
Trodden, yet lingering
Harnessed by Love
For her soon to be
Abandoned children

Leaning gently
Pulled by her trolley
Mother and professor
Teacher to her son
A late night lesson
Nurturing her
Beloved elder
The Heir Apparent

Destined to care for
His helpless siblings

Spirits arching
Silhouettes dreadfully marching
Quieted shadows
At a death enhancing pace
Slowly piping them
Item by item
Through the aisles

Back aching torture
        Just like her
Feet dragging gently
        Just like her
Somber march
        Stepping in unison

Shipwrecked framework
Barely bones
Creeping towards
Her end of days

Respectfully
He followed
Sadly, Bravely
Bowed head
For her
For Him
For the younger
Three comrades

In all
A midnight
Cram session
Solitary forked trail
Leading an inclined
Mind bending journey

No learning curve
Lesson to last a lifetime

Pivotal witness
Eternally circular
Forever enduring

Timeless
Ageless…

Instantaneous!

DEFENCE OF GORGEOUS

Stay close
By my side
Looks like trouble
Straight ahead

Don’t twitch
Don’t blink
If possible
Don’t think

You have
A choice
To be here
But I don’t

UNION DUES

Gather around
A heartfelt meeting
Shallow pomp
Elaborate speeches
Glorious pageantry

Tell the people
We the people
Face the cause

We will trot
Our way
To the highest floor
Stepping in unison
For greater
Stronger alliance

So we
March-March-March
To the
Top-Top-Top
And we
Step-Step-Step
All the way

And we
Knock-Knock-Knock
On the door
For opportunity
And when it opens
We sound the cry

*   *   *   *   *

Regal entry
Long awaited opening
A startled
Genuine leader
Sincerely gesturing
Off the cuff
On the wall
Off to battle

We had demands
Now we stood

And I
Their fearless leader
They at my back
Attack formation
Requested gently
Then firmly insisting
Finally demanding
We want justice

He gave
An awkward look
Leaning forward
Head tilting
Towards my back
Asking curiously…

We???

I turned
And looked
And of the
Twenty or so
That followed me…

…There were none!

SMOKIN' BETSY

Rugged and aged
Back-fire engaged!
Loud sounding
Smoke rusted
Chariot!

Just needed a ride
Father's joy and pride
His beloved
His revered
Smokin' Betsy!

I admit
Now and then
Against backgrounds
Of modern trends
Towards the pious
Encompassing
Pretentious elitist

Slighted emotion
I knew all along
Class was waste
Taste was wrong

Soon I too esteemed
That barreling sound
Of a noisy
Bossy

Guzzling
Old reliable
Queen…

Of the Jalopies

WHY?

I found a book
About Gwendolyn Brooks
At the public Library
Near home

No poetic intent
Even way back then
Yet I craved
My desire to unravel

Back to school
Off to search
The aisles and the shelves
Endless lists of
Encompassing anthologies

But I never
Found her
And I could not understand
Why

Encyclopedias
In every section
Volume after volume
Collection to selection

But she
Nor her name
Could be found

Nowhere in sight
In this Sacred, Holy
Revered Institution

The Best Modern Poets
She wasn't there
The World's Literary Greatest
She wasn't there
Best Beloved Poems
Nowhere to be seen
Everywhere I looked
I could not find her

She was not mentioned
Not even in passing

Not her whit
Not her intellect
Not her prize

LIFELONG TORMENT

The unwritten rule
About apologies
Offer them as soon
As you can

No prior knowledge
To what each hour holds
Every word
Is a bridge
Spanning rivers.

Obscure tool
Often sealed
Silences quivering lips
A quenchless urge
To free
The vines of
Piercing twisted
Relations.

Failure to practice
Time passing
Followed by destiny
Eventually life itself

Eternal hollowness
Ageless passion
Lifelong torment.

THE KITE

All day long
A losing fight
A wasted hurricane holiday
Battling an unruly kite

Furious winds
Breezes of confusion
We knew all the tricks
About newspapers and sticks
Flour and water
And string.

Tie on the tail
A hoist and a sail
But over and again
A botched flight
Fallen membranes
Painfully crashing
To the ground

Failed skyward thrust
Juvenile disgust
We tried everything
Gave our all
Ran full length
Straight into
The mid afternoon

After almost all day
We knew
Our travails
Were hardly
Worth spending

Time wasted
Lost in illusion
Absolute dejection

He appeared
Unexpected
Early arrival
Looked at our mess
Undid a little
Redid a lot
Retied, untwisted
Same string on
Added a good bit more tail

Then came
Those joyous words

TRY IT NOW!
WORK TOGETHER!

Set sail
We ran
With everything we had
This was our final try
At our vacation

And it soared!
High and far
Dancing
Swaying
Almost reaching
The peak

Of our jubilation.

TEACHER'S PET

I'll never forget
The teacher's pet
Always slobbering for
Love and affection

Perfect gloat
Every perfect day
Excessive overkill
To make that "A"

Our taunting
Caught teacher's attention
Our earned reward
A week of detention!

OLE RUPE

This was the night
My father and I
Went to the Monastery
To talk…

About school
About progress
About future

This should be easy
Well natured Nuns
No need for panic
Relax
All will be fine.

Great foyer
Of elegance
Filled to capacity
The rich
The famous
The poor

Chartered to warm
Quieted cubicles
To whisper
And whimper
As necessary.
She was jubilant

Hooded reverence
Carting us merrily along
Down the list
Emphasis on this
Oh look at that!
Happy and bubbling
Shoveling
Kind words with passion
To satisfy our minds

Boldly
Coldly
Suddenly
He stopped her –

UNACCEPTABLE!

Bubble
Bursting
Paused
We both dazed
Then, her mumbled response
To which he again
Exclaimed

UNACCEPTABLE!

He ranted
And raged
Page after page
Giving us looks

As he flipped
Sheet by sheet

A humiliating
Devastating result

My decision
Right there
Right then
Never ever
Ever again

Expect
Or earn
The word

UNACCEPTABLE!

PART III

BOTTOM LINE

Can you tell me,
What is the bottom line?
Please instruct me
How far to go

I'll stand for our cause
Embrace the highest standards
Believe in what you desire
All that you envision

If you want me to be cut throat
I don't do cut throat
But I will if you give me no choice
However, be forewarned:
You don't want me in that position

A journeyman's journey
No desired intentions
Just a definitive point in the right direction
No need for vagueness
No necessity for sojourning endeavors

Just
Plainly
Simply
Tell me
About the bottom line.

HEARTSTRING

[for Crystal]

You are
My precious
Heartstring
From way back
When you were
In the womb

I read to you
Listened
And cuddled
Sang to you
Long before
You were born

On arrival
I cradled
And kissed you

As you grew
You were showered
With hugs

Now all
Fully grown
You're never alone

You will always
Be my
Precious
Heartstring

HALLOWED CAVITY

Oh dreadful sight
Depressing sigh
Amidst bleak wayward ages
Quietly hovering
Over a once saturated
Fading terrain

A cool painful
Echoing deafening silence
Broken by the driven sound
Of crushing gravel
Continuous, monotonous
Pulling, rolling
In the direction of
A hallowed cavity

Blackened despair
Temporal sympathy
A low crawling soul
In search of
Recently beheld
Perfect unison

THE RUDDER

Today my life
Is out of control
Aimless
Without direction

Tireless angry trails
Uneasy waiting
Sweltering
Long term anxiety
For wisdom
To show her compassion

Today my feet
Became motionless
Afraid to move
Step ahead or behind
To the left
To the right
A terrible fight
Internal destructive confusion

Nevertheless
I start prodding along
In a straight path
With blurred details
Encompassed by
An invisible wall
Which cloaks an
Invincible rudder

RAGE OF FOOLS

Never allow anyone
To drive you to rage
Bring your life
Your breath
To despondence

Endlessly idle
Seeking companionship
Clinging to someone
Or something with terrible intent

Unworthy commitment
Spiraling down
At an alarming rate

First the flashing
Then the fleet
Silver cuffs
Stomping cleats
Followed by the clang
Of the cell gates

Distant rustling of keys
Slamming the door
Dimming the light
To your future.

MIND SPIN

My mother died
Last night
And my whole world
Just kept
Spinning
And spinning
And spinning

No neglect
Many paid their respect
Showed compassion
Love and regard

Burdened march
Humming songs
Swinging
Swaying
By tens
By hundreds

Typical dismay
People die every day

Central shattered
Isolated
Oblivious
Domestic domain

My mother died
Last night
And my head just kept
Spinning
And spinning
And spinning

WASTELAND

I have a friend
Who lives in Wasteland
Oblivious to the world around

Taking for granted
Nurtured provisions
Deliberate
Abusive
Entrapment

Uncanny destruction
Strange version of green
Conniving
Unconvincing
Generated
From the root

No known measure
For the residents
Of Wasteland
Use a little
Throw a lot
Destroy as you go

Stumbling

Through a rotted garden of
New earthen flowerbeds

THE PAUPER

There's something
To love
About
Being poor
Each day a new
Lost battle

Mediocre or small
Hounded
Grounded
Lame and defeated
A morbid read story

Recurring
Nightmarish obituary
Scattering one's own ashes
Before the faces
Of illegitimate pseudos
Unable to bear their own shame

Ships without passages
Whip their eye lashes
Sharply
Treacherously

Another war
Another wound
A subtle
Acknowledgement
Of who we are

LOVE OF HATRED

It's so easy to say
Blessed are ye
Yet strive
To run
From such
Endowments

To be hated
To be poor
Are blessings
Bestowed
Upon the choicest
Most beloved
From the Highest

GIMME DAT

Everything
They see
Gimme dis
Gimme dat
Whatever
Their ears hear
They want

Each lingering
Moment
All inclusive

They want yours
They want theirs
They take mine

One day soon
They'll awake
And feel
The startling impact
Of years
Corroded and destroyed

Nature's annoyance
Instinctive response
Against a weary
Exhausting collective

Of
Gimme
Gimme
Gimme

That's all they ever say

Gimme this!
Gimme that!
Gimme those!

MOODY

I don't believe in friendship
I don't believe in love
Back off
Go away
Leave me alone!

Yesterday
We were friends
Nothing has changed
Except
I don't want
To be bothered!

Stop wasting time
Trying to figure
Out my mind
Attempting to snuggle
Your way
Next to me

Step back!
Stay away!
Pack and go home!

Tomorrow
Perhaps
Things will renew

Well…
Wait…

Maybe…
I do believe in friendship

And…
Maybe…
I do believe in love

Just…

Not today!

SEARCH FOR TRUTH

Tomorrow
When I wake up
I'll search for truth
Won't stop
Until I find it.

Purge my mind
Of pre-arranged concepts
Hollowed brain
Resonating moderately
Vacancy seeking wisdom
Waiting for words.

To cloth
Now barren
Forestry.

RAT STANDARD

Place both feet firmly
Before the great obtuse
Breath enhanced
Starter race stance
Perfect challenge
For the sprint to the top

A seasonal tailored pace
Ruled along an irreverent yardstick
With inconsistent
Double or triple standards
By incoherent design

Unwholesome
Immeasurable
Sliding rule

Against
A friend
A foe
An unassuming
Accomplice

Unaware
Unafraid
All alone

A perfect prey

THE INNOCENT ONE

All alone
In a darkened cell
Metallic numbing cold
Brands and bruises
Of an innocent man

Muffled soft echoes
Like caged unicorns
Sounding for freedom
A maddening dash
Towards a daunting freefall

The humbled voice
Of this
Model for naught
Roving light rays
Howling winds
Torment this
Bargain for destruction

Tagged and ticketed
Involuntary participant
Rolling to the beat of a
Repeating drum line

Rigid confusion
Legal inhibitions
Guilty of being accused

SURPRISE

Did you hear?
What they said?
When we stumbled that night
Onto a sight
Too wild to believe!

Of you know what
And you know where
And we heard when
Whatever happened!

I'll tell you the details
Of passion and poise
How shame and disgrace
Brew from glory.

I'll start with a hint
No subtle intent…

…My, my,
..You're a tid bit
...Too nosy!

TRIALS OF ANNA

The news came slowly
She had gradually
Lost her eyesight
Grief more to me
Than challenge
To her

How would she cope?
Once common rituals
Now daily
Weighted routines

Further
How would he endure?
Dragging along
With minimum functionality
Abject misery
My poor mind

And so I began
My worn saddened
Well rehearsed journey
Back home
To see my bedridden mother
Cared for by a
Helplessly
Dependent father

* * * * * *

Suddenly
The sound of pans
Awaken the sunrise
Clanging and fussing
The sounds of harmonious
Contentious marriage

Hurry get my clothes!

Those aren't what
I prepared for you!
Take that shirt off!

Blind
She patted
The heating iron
And joyfully pressed
His wrinkled shirt

Hurry, I need to go!
Oh sit down and be quiet
Stop rushin' and fussin'
You can't go out
'Till I finish fixing your food

Click on the stove
Heating pots and pans
Simmer some sunny side
Grits, bacon and coffee
Butter smothered toast
Meal for a king

Puzzled…

I peered
At this curious pair

My misconception
Father's advantageous despair

I closed my eyes
And listened to see
Two blind
Happy people

And a blinder me.

TRAVELLING TEACHERS

Warriors travel
And challenge
The world

The ordinary
Return home
To comfort

PART IV

FATHOM

It's difficult
To understand
Destruction

To justify
Erring ways

Pillage
Plunder

All for self justification
Barbaric entrapment
Conventional clause

Death of enemies
Death of innocents
Death even to self

It's hard
To comprehend
To fathom
The mental state
And…

The well stated

Innate intent
To eliminate
Mankind

TELL ME

Tell me
Where are we going?
Stop and pause
For a while

Break neck speed
Standing on the gas peddle
Blazing trails
To where?

Humongous rush
Accelerating pace
Aggregate attitude
Epitomized altitude

Got to right this ship
Healthy and sound
Map the uncharted
Turn things around

But, please tell me
Where are we going?
How and when
Will we get there?

LAPSE

A
Momentary
Lapse

Forgot
What happened
Don't remember
Can't recall
The circumstances

The occurrence…
The record…

Control
Alt
Delete

A digital brain
How convenient

SHAKEDOWN

Who do they think they are?
That's what folk always say.

Not with their lips
But with their hearts
Their minds
And their eyes

Just a good old
Hometown
Wake up

Bold words
They sound like they
Understand what they're saying

Brave walk
They strut like they
Know where they're heading

Smooth suave
They act like they
Enjoy what they're doing

But pay no mind…

Just another nobody
Who doesn't know anyone
No connections
Whatsoever!

Go ahead
Put on a show!
Time for a
Good old fashioned

Shakedown!

Rattle that cage!
Ring that bell
LOUD!

See if anyone
Comes to the rescue

But caution…

If they are
Indeed
Knowledgeable

Or even worse
If they somehow
Do know somebody

And by chance
And the passing of time

This "someone"
Gets to where they're going

Don't be
At all
Surprised…

Look out…

Put on your
Shakin' shoes

It's time for
The real…

SHAKEDOWN!

LAW OF LOVE

[for Bev]

Remember
When our eyes met
We instantly knew love
Springing from your spirit
Flowing through my heart

Enlightened angel
Eclectic dancing rays
Streaming, beaming
Against our fading
Monochromatic sanctuary

Choirs gracefully caroling
Viols and symphonies
Perfectly tuned
Elegance
Orchestrated from above

The moment
Our hearts met
I fell deep in love

JUGULAR SOCIETY

Lingering
Quiet rainy day
Splish, splash
Got to get his young hands
On a little playful cash

He was supposed to stay home
Mind Ressa and Macy
Now, what is this?

Something happened
Something big
This is not about some teacher calling
No minor neighborhood complaint

Must have done
Something incredibly awful
Really, really, bad

Blue light flashing
Cops crashing
Bursting through the door
Waving their warrant
Babies crying

Momma's
Gonna be upset
Then disgusted
Then totally angry
About whatever happened

About him leaving
Those children alone

Half a mile away
Drizzling rain
Chill in the air
Bones shivering
World of rigid
Freezing concrete
Adjacent to
Course wet asphalt

What is this?
Laying lifeless
On the bare sidewalk

Stiff

Rain mingled with
Warm cooling
Red streaming stains

Breeze gently blowing
Frequently exposing
A haunting horrified
Gasping last glance.

My, my, my
What on earth is this?
Who could have done this?
And look…
Is that a…
Bullet hole in his side?

What kind of person?...
What type of human?...
Would?...

Even if some…
Trivial wrong…
Was committed…
Who could do this,
To a fifteen year old?

Need to go
Into that store
Talk to Mr. Charlie…
Got to have a word.
Must have my say
Right is right
Wrong is wrong
But this is too much.

No way.
No way!
No way!!

Bend to enter
Debris covered floor
Shattered glass everywhere
Each step
Crushing bits of
Hollow warnings
Down the aisle
Each step slower
Sensing reality
Bad bad feeling

Almost there
Something isn't right

Oh my goodness
Look at Mr. Charlie
Look at Mr. Charlie

Sitting up straight
Staring into nothingness
Peaceful face
Grimacing gash
Targeted at the heart
Not truly at him
But at his benefactors
Not Mr. Charlie
Please not Mr. Charlie

Came into our community
When nobody else would
Began to form relationships
When no one else thought we all could

Who will care for his children?
Who will calm his wife?

Now look at him
How could this be?

…What kind of…

MONSTER...
Would do this?

LEGALLY ILLEGAL

we filled out the forms
because it was the law

we stood in long lines
because it was required

we paid ridiculous fees
because they forced us to

we were humiliated
they treated us terribly

mentally shaken
from this ugly mess
travelling
along the very
fringes of sanity

we entered
we lived
in a new familiar territory

barren communications
within long established
predictable estates

searching for a trail
envisioning
peaceful lodging

desiring warmth
from an earnest
most basic domain

ours
was a license
to migrate

theirs…

a license to ensure
that we did so

miserably

THE MACHINERY

In awe of
The machinery
Monstrous sized gears
Rotating slothful axis
Decrepit rusted eras

Isometric
Frontal tilted elevation
Exceedingly intimidating

Why bother try
Inevitable asphyxiation
Eventual doom

But we are designed
With desire
To challenge
To dream
To dare

Create
Communicate
Manufacture

Even
Foolishly talk
About

Change

Change?

From what
To what?

Or is it all about specifications
And process?

And
EVERYBODY
Knows

People
Who know
ANYTHING
About specifications
And process

Seldom

IF EVER
Utter the word

CHANGE!

NOWHERELAND

Got up early this morning
Put on my suit and shoes
Started singing and dancing
Time to share the good news

Tweaked my presentation
Rolled up my plans
Look Momma I'm heading
To Nowhereland!

Nothing in my pocket
Nothing in my head
On with the show
Forge straight towards the unseen

Never mind about studying
Wasted struggling and grueling
Earn your keep?
Who do they think they're fooling?

Suddenly stalled on the pathway
No way to win
Except to start over again
And do it right this time

Early next morning
No suit no show
No singing or dancing
Just time for a fresh beginning.

PART V

SOCIOPOLITICAL POETRY

"We are all born into situations,
We are forced to bump and hop;
People make the world go wrong
People, make it stop!"

BORN TO DIE
(10,000 FUNERALS)

Gonna buy my boy a suit,
To attend
His father's
Funeral;

Gonna buy my boy
Ten thousand suits
To attend
Ten thousand
Funerals.

We are all born into situations,
We are forced to bump and hop;
People make the world go wrong;
People! Make it stop!

I see a little black boy,
Ambitious, incomplete;
Another Hemmingway,
Einstein,
Riddled in the street.

No matter how hard you struggle,
No matter how loud you shout;
The whole world by design,
Don't let no Negro out.

There are those who may succeed,
But they're merely little pawns;

And if you dare look close;
We're really little toms.

Reach down and touch your baby,
He now is fully grown;
Look down and shed a tear,
He'll never know his own.

No matter how hard you foster,
No matter how much you give;
A black man's born to die,
Before he starts to live.

Gonna buy my boy a suit,
To attend
His father's
Funeral;

Gonna buy my boy
Ten thousand suits,
To attend
Ten thousand
Funerals.

BAHAMIAN DEMOCRACY

"Know Your Station"

Nobody tells anybody what to do,
Nobody tells anybody what not to do;
No one tells anyone what to say,
No one tells anyone what not to say.

Anyone who does not know what to do;
And does what they ought not do, and,
Anyone who does not know what to say;
And says something they should not say…

Is made into an example;
Beaten into the dirt;
Taken to the cleaners;
Hung out to dry;
For all to see,
And know…

Everyone should know what to do;
Everyone should know what not to do;
Everybody should know what to say;
Everybody should know what not to say.

This is Bahamian Democracy.
KNOW YOUR STATION!

THE RETALIATION

[July 28, 2006]

There are gonna be days,
You'll forget;
There are gonna be times,
You won't remember;
Our lives,
Snatched away;
Given up freely for you.

Our Country cries each Mother's Day;
Four Heroes died, the 10th of May;
Loyal to the end.

Remember to cry, cry in memoriam;
Remember to shed a tear,
For four brave long lost sons;
And if your soul gets weak,
Call on Jesus,
His Name is written in our law.

Edward, bear the armor;
Fenrick, man the gun;
Aim towards my Bahama sea line;
Aim towards our setting sun.

Tell our sons and daughters,
Stand for justice, wear you pride;
Don’t believe “El Revolución,”
The truth was told the day Flamingo died.

FREEDOM SONG

If your way gets weary
Think of Martin
He’ll be standing
By your side

Singin' la la ha de da
La ha de da ha
La la la la
Oh oh oh

Thank you
For doing your duty

If you're dancin' in the dark
Set your heart on Rosa Parks
She sat down
And we rode our way to freedom

If you're singin' freedom's song
Set your mind on Andrew Young
By design he’s close
To Jimmy Carter Boulevard

Feel the joy
Hear the news
Down from Auburn Avenue
Albernathy, Coretta and Hosea

All the Prophets from long ago
Jerusalem to Jericho
Moses, Isaac and Abraham
From John the Baptist to The Great I Am

Lord you strengthened them
To do their duty.

As our world spirals down,
Global leaders seem to be confounded;
Help them Lord
To do their duty.

Teach us all Lord;
To do our duty.

SONG OF THE EXILE

Innocent objective
Trek down the isle
Marriage to misfortune
Long harrowing cry
Heartbeat by heartbeat
Step by frightening step
Battle of a lifetime
Opponents unknown
Riding chariots
Laden with
Resources unlimited

First time contender
Bureaucrat of the first order
Future politician
Diplomat to the heart
Corrupt to the core

They called him
Mr. Luthie
And I met him
Face to face
Little did I know
I was breaking the ranks

Scholarships were reserved
For the higher ups
Relatives and friends
Of Politicians
Permanent Secretaries

And those who
Found their favor

Puritanical naiveté
Filling out forms
Rubbing those people
The wrong way
Trying to take
What was rightfully theirs
A cherished jewel
Their tax
Supported
Birthright.

Offended?
They were furious
In totality.

My take was innocent
Different
Difficult
For me to comprehend
For them to fathom

Dutifully paid my taxes
Levied the Customs dues
This was my democratic
Right;

To stand in line
Wait my turn
And fill out
My application

To have it stamped…

REJECTED!

Further,
Rejection
Then…
Absolute disgust.

Finally, way out of line!
A pitiful
Miserable nobody
Attempting to usurp
Their rightful inheritance
Stealing their public documents
Filling out their forms.

Then came the barrage
Hidden assaults
Disguised amongst
Friends
Enemies
Amidst heated "discussions"
Of what was theirs
What will always be theirs
And what's was supposedly public.

Year in
Year out
Beaten long and low
Should have thrown
In the towel
A long long time back

But…
Something kept me going;
Just scraping to survive

Then at last
One day
It finally happened

They made a mistake
A humongous error
Of judgment
Of rudiments
Of the first order
Revealing their true ugliness

Youthful assertion
Killer instincts
Kicked in
Crossed every "t"
Dotted every "i"
Marched down
To the Embassy
To lodge an
Informal complaint

I wasn't stupid
Mr. Ambassador
Used to be a
Card carrying member
Of the
You know who

You know why
You know where
And you know when.

Like Captain Moxey
Used to say
My mother
May have given birth
To one or two fools
But I absolutely
Positively
Beyond a shadow of doubt
Guarantee you
I wasn't one of them.

Long story short
Disadvantage
Became
Advantage

And
Refracted
Disadvantage
Transformed to

EXILE.

WHY ARE THEY CRYING?

I was born
of a lonely town
Where they ate
and lived
Seems like forever

But now
I'm almost certain
They're about
to close the curtain

Won't you tell me
Please tell me

Why are they crying?
Please tell me why
Why are they crying?

They never hate
or hurt anybody
They only used
For needed survival

But now
I'm almost certain
They're about
to close the curtain

Won't you tell me
Won't you tell me

Please tell me
Why are they crying?

Please tell me why
Why are they crying?

THE LAST STRAW

Early sunrise
Rush to the bus stop
Reach the Straw Market
Time to make a living

Up late last night
Finally done
Just in time
For the sale of a basket
Just in time
To start over again

From manufacturing
To production
Marketing and design
This merchant was running
Her own assembly line

Such were the trials
Of a struggling straw vendor
Grateful
Thankful
For her blessings
Living in the shadows of grace.

Bending from burdens
Hopping high hurdles
Always with a smile.

When the record is set
Of things said and done
We bear witness
To a humble soul

The last laughter
The last cry
The last orphan she fed

The last song
The last glance
The last scripture she read

The last place that she went
Her last statement of faith
The last dollar she placed
On the offering plate.

The last weave
The last walk
Her last bump
Her last flaw,

The last sleep
The last dream
The last breath
The last straw.

ABOUT THE AUTHOR

Sam "SIP SIP" Williams has been writing poetry since his early teenage years, and in this the second edition of his first book, he has compiled a collection of poetry and prose which highlight his childhood challenges.

Born Rupert Samuel Williams, Jr., he is from the Bahamas, and writes primarily from his life's experiences, using his background as a visual artist and as both a professional engineer and a registered architect, to identify and convey beautiful technical poetic mind challenging concepts.

In addition to writing poetry, Mr. Williams also writes essays and articles for publication for a Christian magazine. He owns a small engineering firm, and is an award-winning political cartoonist.

He resides with his wife, Beverly, in Atlanta, Georgia, and is the proud father of four adult children and eight grandchildren.

www.ingramcontent.com/pod-product-compliance
Lightning Source LLC
Chambersburg PA
CBHW020524310726
48979CB00014B/2198/J
* 9 7 8 0 9 8 1 6 4 2 4 4 4 *